HANSEL and GRETEL

Modern Publishing
A Division of Unisystems, Inc. / New York, New York 10022

Once upon a time, a brother and sister named Hansel and Gretel lived in a small cottage with their father and stepmother. The family was very poor.

Hansel and Gretel's father was kind and loving, but their stepmother was mean and hateful. She made sure Hansel and Gretel had chores to do from morning until night, and she scolded them all the time.

"Spill one drop of water from that bucket and you'll go to bed without supper!" she would shout as Gretel carried heavy buckets of water from the well.

One night, the woman said to her husband, ''We are poor and hardly have enough food to feed all of us, and those children are lazy and worthless. Let us lead them into the forest and leave them there. They will find another home and another family, who will have more to spare than we do.''

Hansel and Gretel's father was very sad, but he thought that if his children could find a better life somewhere else he ought to let them go. He decided to do as his wife said and leave the children in the middle of the forest, unable to find their way home.

Hansel and Gretel heard every word, and Gretel was frightened.

"Don't worry," Hansel whispered. "I have a plan." Later that night, he slipped outside and gathered as many pebbles as he could find.

The next day, as the children followed their father and stepmother into the forest, Hansel dropped the pebbles one by one.

Sure enough, when their parents left them, the children followed the trail of pebbles back home.

Their stepmother was furious. She locked them in their room so they couldn't gather more pebbles for the next day when she and her husband would again leave them in the forest.

In the morning, Hansel did not eat his slice of bread for breakfast. Instead, he broke it up and left a trail of crumbs.

But by nightfall, the birds had eaten every crumb! Hansel and Gretel could not find their way home.

That night, the children slept in the forest.
When Hansel woke, he smelled something delicious.

Hansel and Gretel followed the scent. It led to a gingerbread house decorated with candy and frosting! They began to eat.

Scarcely had the children taken a bite when they heard a voice cackle, "Stop eating my house!"

They turned to see a very ugly old witch. "We're sorry," said Gretel. "We were hungry and didn't know it was your house!"

"Sorry are you?" snickered the witch. "Not as sorry as you're going to be!" She dragged the children behind the house and locked Hansel up in a wooden box with iron bars.

"Your brother will stay in there, while you work for me!" growled the witch. "Every day he will eat and eat, and when he is fat enough I will roast him up and have him for supper!"

Gretel worked hard while Hansel remained locked up. Each day, the witch would check to see how fat he had gotten.

"Hold out your finger so that I can tell how plump it is!" she ordered.

But the witch was nearly blind, so clever Hansel would hold out a chicken bone instead of his finger. Day after day, she waited for Hansel to get fatter.

Finally, she had waited long enough. "If the oven's hot, I'm going to roast you right now!" cried the evil witch.

The witch leaned over to see if the oven was hot. Gretel pushed the witch right into the oven and slammed the door!

Gretel grabbed the key and freed Hansel. Then, together they searched the witch's house to see what they could find.

Much to their surprise, they discovered a chest full of jewels!

"We can find our way home in the daylight," Gretel told Hansel, "and we will take these jewels with us so that our family will never be poor again!"

When the children reached home, they learned
that their stepmother had run away.

"Don't worry, Father," said Hansel. "As long
as we three are together, we will live happily
for the rest of our lives!"